Disney · PIXAR

The Junior Novelization

Library of Congress Control Number: 2008930603

ISBN: 978-0-7364-2584-1

www.randomhouse.com/kids

Printed in the United States of America

10 9 8   First Edition

DISNEY · PIXAR

The Junior Novelization

Adapted by Jasmine Jones

Random House New York

Chapter 1

Young Carl Fredricksen sat in the darkened movie theater, wearing his leather flight helmet. He straightened in his seat as a newsreel flickered onto the screen. The newsreels were Carl's favorite part of going to the movies. They were full of information about people, places, and exciting events going on in the world.

"Movietown News presents . . . 'Spotlight on the Rich'!" came the voice of the announcer. "Our subject today: Charles Muntz."

Carl leaned forward. Charles Muntz was a famous adventurer—and Carl's hero.

"The beloved aviation pioneer lands his dirigible, the *Spirit of Adventure,* in New Hampshire this week, completing a yearlong expedition into the lost world! This lighter-than-air craft was designed by Muntz himself. And what has Muntz brought back this time?"

The black-and-white film showed an enormous blimp landing in an open field. Then Muntz appeared on the screen. He looked tall and handsome in a leather jacket and a flight helmet just like Carl's.

"Adventure is out there!" Muntz exclaimed into the camera. He lowered his goggles over his eyes and gave a thumbs-up.

Carl lowered his goggles, too, wishing he were a grown-up. Then he could go have some adventures, just like Charles Muntz, traveling all over the world, discovering new things, and bringing back priceless treasures.

"Gentlemen, I give you the Monster of Paradise Falls!" Muntz exclaimed on the movie screen. A curtain next to him dropped, revealing the skeleton of a giant bird. It was Muntz's latest discovery.

"But what's this?" the announcer said. "The National Explorers Society accuses Muntz of fabricating the skeleton!"

Carl watched, horrified, as the Explorers Society removed Muntz's photo from its Wall of Fame. *How can the Explorers Society doubt Muntz?* Carl thought. *He's the greatest explorer of all!*

But Muntz didn't give up. "I promise to capture the beast . . . alive!" he cried on the flickering screen. "And I will not come back until I do."

Carl smiled as the crowd around him cheered. *Adventure is out there, all right,* Carl thought. He just knew it.

Later that afternoon, Carl was still thinking about Muntz. He'd written SPIRIT OF ADVENTURE on the side of a balloon, and as he ran, he pretended the balloon was his airship. He buzzed and zoomed, making the kinds of noises he thought a blimp might make.

"Adventure is out there!" said a voice, seemingly from nowhere.

Carl stopped in his tracks. *Who said that?* he wondered. When he looked up, he realized that he was standing in front of an abandoned house.

Something creaked. Carl looked up and saw that someone had attached a rope to the weather vane on top of the house. The rope tugged at the weather vane, turning it.

"Look out!" cried the voice from inside the house. "Mount Rushmore. Must get *Spirit of Adventure* over Mount Rushmore. Hard to starboard. Hold together, old girl. *Whew!* How're my dogs doing? *Ruff, ruff . . . ruff!* Good boy!"

Carl crept toward the porch. SPIRIT OF ADVENTURE was written across the front door. He squeezed past the door. When he saw what was inside, his eyes widened in surprise. Pictures of Charles Muntz were tacked to the wall. Adventure gear was everywhere—ropes, a compass, even an old bicycle. A girl stood near the front window, "steering" with the wheel of the upside-down bike. She was wearing a leather helmet like Carl's and looking out the window. "All engines ahead full!" she commanded. "Let's take her up twenty-six thousand feet!"

There was no doubt about it—this girl was playing adventurer, too. Carl turned to get a better look at her collection of Charles Muntz photos and newspaper clippings.

"What are you doing?" the girl asked, suddenly appearing at his side.

Carl let out a yelp. He was so surprised that he let go of his balloon.

"Don't you know that this is an exclusive club?" the girl demanded. "Only explorers get in here. Not just any kid off the street with a helmet and a pair of goggles. Do you think you got what it takes? Well, do you?"

Carl stammered.

"All right, you're in," said the girl. "Welcome aboard." She held out her hand, but Carl didn't take it. He found the girl a bit intimidating.

"What's wrong?" she asked, more gently. "Can't you talk? Hey, I don't bite."

The girl took off her helmet and shook out her messy red hair. Buttons and badges were pinned to the front of her shirt. She unfastened one made out of the cap from a bottle of grape soda. "You and me, we're in a club now," she said, pinning the cap onto Carl's shirt.

Carl smiled, and the girl grinned back.

"I saw where your balloon went," she said, looking up toward the second story. "Come on, let's go get it."

The girl quickly walked out of the room, heading for the creaky old staircase in the hallway. Carl didn't move. He was still feeling stunned.

Half a second passed. Then the girl popped back in with a quizzical look on her face. Clearly, she was wondering why Carl hadn't followed. Then she grinned, realizing what the problem must be. She had forgotten to introduce herself!

"My name's Ellie," she said cheerfully. Carl's face turned bright red as she grabbed his hand and pulled him into the hall.

Together the two picked their way up the stairs. Carl followed Ellie, careful to tread in her exact footsteps. He didn't want to fall through the rotten wood.

At the top, Ellie took Carl's hand and helped him over the last step. Carl blushed, but Ellie didn't notice. "There it is," she said, pointing to the balloon. Unfortunately, it was floating in a room that didn't have a floor. A single beam stretched across the empty space.

Carl gulped. It was a twelve-foot drop to the floor below.

"Well, go ahead," Ellie urged.

Carl screwed up his courage and stepped onto the beam. He took another step, inching forward.

He was halfway across when he felt the beam splinter. He had just enough time to see the shocked look on Ellie's face before he fell.

Carl propped up the flashlight with his good arm. He was trying to read in bed, but it wasn't too comfortable. He'd broken his arm when he had fallen off the beam in Ellie's clubhouse.

The curtains fluttered like ghosts as a breeze blew gently across the room. A blue balloon with a stick tied to the end floated in through Carl's window. Carl let out a shriek and jumped, banging his arm against the side table. "Ow!"

A head of messy red hair popped in through the window. "Hey, kid!"

Carl shrieked again and hit himself in the face with his cast. "Ow!"

"Thought you might need a little cheerin' up," Ellie said as she climbed through the window. She joined Carl under the tent he had made with his blankets. "I got something to show you. I am about to let you see something I have never shown to another human being. Ever. In my life." She added, "You'll have to swear you will not tell anyone."

Carl nodded, wide-eyed.

"Cross your heart. Do it."

Carl crossed his heart, and Ellie nodded, satisfied.

"My adventure book," Ellie said, pulling out her homemade scrapbook. She turned to the first page—a photo of Charles Muntz. "You know him. Charles Muntz . . . *explorer*. When I get big, I'm going where he's going—South America." She pointed to a map that was pasted into the book. "It's like America, but *south*. Wanna know where I'm gonna live? Paradise Falls. 'A land lost in time.'" She pointed to a beautiful photo of a *tepui*, a steep, rugged mountain with a flat top. She had drawn a picture of her clubhouse sitting on the tepui, next to the falls. "I ripped this right out of a library book. I'm gonna move my clubhouse there and park it right next to the falls. Who knows what lives up there! And once I get there . . ."

She flipped through the book until she came to a page marked STUFF I'M GOING TO DO. After that, all the pages were blank. "Well, I'm saving these pages for all the adventures I'm gonna have," Ellie explained. "Only, I just don't know how I'm gonna get to Paradise Falls."

Carl glanced up at the shelf that held his collection of toy blimps. His blue balloon floated beside them. Ellie followed his gaze.

"That's it!" she cried. "You can take us there in a blimp! Swear you'll take us. Cross your heart! Cross it! Cross your heart."

Carl crossed his heart.

Ellie heaved a sigh of relief. "Good. You promised. No backing out."

Carl shook his head. No way would he back out. This girl was a *real* adventurer. Look at what had happened today! Carl had spent ten minutes with her, and he'd already had the biggest adventure of his life. If she said she was going to South America, then Carl wanted to go along.

"Well, see you tomorrow, kid!" Ellie chirped happily as she headed toward the window and climbed out. "Bye. Adventure is out there!" She poked her head back in. "You know, you don't talk very much. I like you!" With those parting words, Ellie disappeared into the night.

Carl stared at the empty window for a moment. "Wow," he said, resting his cheek against the top of the balloon.

His balloon popped, as if it completely agreed with him.

Chapter 2

From that moment on, Carl and Ellie were best friends. When they were nineteen, they got married. They moved into Ellie's clubhouse and had fun fixing it up. Ellie hammered shingles onto the roof. Carl put up a new weather vane. Ellie pulled out her old adventure book, and Carl painted the house so that it looked exactly like the clubhouse in Ellie's drawing.

One day, Carl leaned against the mailbox, admiring Ellie's work as she painted their names on the side. But when he pulled back, he gasped. He'd left a handprint in the paint! Ellie smiled and put her hand in the paint, too. When she pulled it away, it looked as if their prints were holding hands.

They worked on the house every day, and the days turned into weeks. Sometimes they took a break. They would sit in two comfy chairs that were placed side by side in the living room. Other times they would climb to the top of their favorite hill and have a picnic. They liked to lie in the grass, stare up at the sky, and watch the clouds transform into different shapes, like turtles and elephants.

Ellie got a job at the local zoo, taking care of the animals in the South America House. Carl worked at the zoo, too. He sold balloons from a cart. Sometimes Carl had so many balloons, the cart would rise right off the ground!

The weeks turned into months. Ellie and Carl looked through her adventure book and dreamed of traveling to Paradise Falls. Ellie painted a lovely picture of their house atop the tepui. They hung the picture over the fireplace. Carl added a poster of South America. Ellie put up a handwoven rug, a piece of pottery, and a figurine of a tropical bird.

For the finishing touch, Carl placed a toy blimp on the mantel and a glass jar on the table. A label on the jar read PARADISE FALLS. Carl and Ellie tossed their spare change into the jar whenever they could.

But they never had much money. And they always seemed to need to spend the money they had—a new tire for the car, a cast for Carl's broken leg, a new roof for the house. But Carl and Ellie didn't worry. They knew they would get to South America someday.

The months turned into years.

Carl sold his balloons, and Ellie cared for the zoo animals. At night, they danced in the living room. They always had fun together.

One day, when they had been married more than thirty years, Carl realized that they had been waiting long enough. He decided to surprise Ellie. He bought two plane tickets to South America and tucked them into a picnic basket. But as they were on the way up their favorite hill, Ellie fell down.

Ellie went to the hospital, and for a while it looked as if she might get better. But she didn't. Instead, Carl went to her funeral with a bouquet of blue balloons.

Then he went home. For the first time since he was eight years old, Carl was completely alone.

The alarm clock buzzed, and Carl searched for his glasses. He sat up in bed, rubbing his face. He was an old man now. *Waking up isn't as easy as it used to be,* he thought as he stretched. His bones creaked and cracked. He grabbed his cane, which had tennis balls stuck to the bottom prongs for traction, and rode his elderly-assistance chair down the staircase. It took Carl a long, long time to get downstairs.

Carl ate breakfast, then puttered around the house. He dusted the mantel above the fireplace, where he and Ellie had collected all their special adventure items. Carl made sure to carefully replace the tropical-bird figurine next to the pair of binoculars and a framed photo of Ellie as a young girl. Then he slowly walked to the front door, put on his hat, and adjusted the grape-soda pin on his lapel. He paused to check his reflection in the mirror before he unlocked all the locks on the front door and walked out to the porch.

The neighborhood had changed over the years. In fact, it wasn't much of a neighborhood anymore. Every other house on the block had been torn down. A construction crew was building new high-rise apartments.

"Quite a sight, huh, Ellie?" Carl said as he watched the bulldozers crawl over the dirt.

Carl knew that Ellie was no longer there to hear him. But he still liked to talk to her sometimes. After all, the house was filled with things they had made together. Everything about it reminded him of her.

Carl's eyes fell on the mailbox. It hadn't changed since the day Ellie had painted it. It still had both their names—and their handprints. A few letters poked from its door.

"Mail's here!" Carl announced. He tottered to the box and pulled out a brochure. Good-looking elderly people smiled up at him from the bright pamphlet. "Shady Oaks Retirement. Oh, brother." Carl noticed that the mailbox was covered with dust. Frowning, he picked up a leaf blower and blew the dust away.

"Hey! Morning, Mr. Fredricksen!" a construction worker named Tom called over to him. "Need any help there?"

"Yes. Tell your boss over there that you boys are ruining our house," Carl growled, glancing over at a businessman talking on his cell phone.

"Well, just to let you know, my boss would be happy to take this old place off your hands, and for *double* his last offer," Tom replied. "What do you say to that?"

In answer, Carl blasted Tom with the leaf blower.

"Uh, I'll take that as a no, then," Tom said.

"I believe I made my position to your boss quite clear," Carl said.

"You poured prune juice in his gas tank," Tom replied.

Carl chuckled. "Oh, yeah, that was good."

"This is serious," Tom said, frowning. "He's out to get your house."

Carl turned and went back up his front steps.

"Tell your boss he can have our house," he called back over his shoulder. "When I'm *dead*!" He slammed the door.

Tom raised his eyebrows. "I'll take that as a maybe."

Inside the house, Carl sat down in his chair and turned on the television.

"If you order right now," said the man on the screen, "you're gonna get the camera. You're gonna get the printer. You're gonna get the . . ." Carl's eyelids felt heavy. His head started to nod.

Just then, someone knocked at the door. Carl got up and shuffled over to answer it.

A boy in a Junior Wilderness Explorer uniform was standing on Carl's porch. He wore a sash covered in badges, and he was holding a Wilderness Explorer handbook. "Good afternoon," the boy read from his handbook, "my name is Russell, and I am a Wilderness Explorer in Tribe Fifty-four, Sweat Lodge Twelve. Are you in need of any assistance today, sir?"

"No," Carl said.

"I could help you cross the street," Russell suggested.

"No."

"I could help you cross your yard."

"No."

"I could help you cross your porch."

"No."

"Well, I've got to help you cross something," Russell insisted.

"Uh, no," Carl said. "I'm doing fine." He shut the door in Russell's face.

Carl stood in the hallway, listening. But he didn't

hear Russell's footsteps walking away. After a moment, he yanked open the door.

"Good afternoon, my name is Russell," Russell repeated, "and I am a Wilderness Explorer in Tribe Fifty-four, Sweat Lodge Twelve. Are you in need of any assistance today, sir?"

"Thank you, but I don't need any help." Carl tried to shut the door, but Russell jammed his hiking boot into the doorframe, blocking it.

"Ow!" Russell winced.

With a sigh, Carl opened the door. Clearly, this kid wasn't going to give up. "Proceed."

"Good afternoon," said Russell, starting over.

"But skip to the end!" Carl snapped.

Russell pointed to his sash. Many colorful patches had been sewn onto it. There was only one space left on the whole sash. "See these?" he asked. "They are my Wilderness Explorer badges. You may notice, one is missing. It's my Assisting the Elderly badge. If I get it, I will become a Senior Wilderness Explorer. The wilderness must be explored!" Russell made his hands into a W. He flapped his hands and squawked like a bird. *"Caw-caw!"* Then Russell's hands became claws as he growled like a bear. *"Rarr!"*

Carl's hearing aid shrieked in his ear.

"It's going to be great," Russell went on. "There's a big ceremony, and all the dads come, and they pin on our badges."

"So you want to assist an old person?" Carl asked.

"Yep! Then I will be a Senior Wilderness Explorer!" Russell grinned.

Carl looked left, then right. Then he leaned in to whisper, "You ever heard of a snipe?"

"Snipe?" Russell shook his head.

"Bird. Beady eyes. Every night, it sneaks into my yard and gobbles my poor azaleas. I'm elderly and infirm; I can't catch it. If only someone could help me."

"Me!" Russell bounced up and down with excitement. "Me! I'll do it!"

"Oh, I don't know," Carl said doubtfully, "it's awfully crafty. You'd have to clap your hands three times to lure it in."

"I'll find it, Mr. Fredricksen!" Russell promised.

"I think its burrow is two blocks down. If you go past—"

But Russell was already on the case. "Two blocks down! Got it!" He hurried away, clapping and calling, "Sni-i-i-pe. Here, snipey, snipey!"

"Bring it back here when you find it!" Carl shouted.

That should keep him busy for a while, Carl thought. He knew something that Russell didn't: There was no snipe. He'd made it up.

Carl started to close his door, but the beeping sound of a large truck backing up caught his attention. One of the construction workers was directing the truck—and it was headed right toward Carl's mailbox!

Crunch!

"Hey!" Moving faster than he had in years,

Carl picked up his cane and hurried toward the mailbox. "Hey, you!" he hollered at the construction worker. "What do you think you're doing?"

"I am so sorry, sir." The worker really did look sorry. He bent over to try to fix the mailbox.

"Don't touch that!" Carl barked, reaching for it.

"No, no, no," the worker said. "Let me take care of that for you."

Carl struggled to keep his grip on the box. The construction worker didn't understand. To him, it was just a mailbox. But to Carl, it was *Ellie's* mailbox. The one she had painted. The one with their handprints. "Get away from our mailbox!" Carl warned.

"Hey, sir, I—"

"I don't want you to touch it!" Carl cried. He batted at the construction worker with his cane.

"Ow!" The worker fell to the ground, holding his head.

Carl cradled the mailbox in his arms and retreated to the house. His heart was thudding in his chest. He hadn't realized that he was still strong enough to hurt another person. People had gathered around to make sure the construction worker was okay. A few glanced nervously at Carl.

Quickly, Carl went inside the house and shut the front door. He also closed the curtains, but kept one open a little so he could peek out. He saw a police car roll up beside the crowd of people. The real estate boss was there, too, and he was staring right at Carl. Scared, Carl pulled away from the window. He knew he'd made a mistake. A big mistake.

Chapter 3

"Sorry, Mr. Fredricksen. You don't seem like a public menace to me." The police officer smiled apologetically as she dropped Carl off at his front door. Carl had just spent the entire day in court. The judge had ruled that Carl was guilty of assaulting the construction worker.

"Take this." The officer handed Carl a brochure for Shady Oaks Retirement Village. "The guys from Shady Oaks will be by to pick you up in the morning, okay?"

Carl heard the police car drive away. He looked down at the cheerful, good-looking people in the brochure. The judge had said that Carl couldn't live by himself anymore. He didn't have to go to jail— but he did have to go to a retirement home.

To Carl, that was just as bad. He didn't want to leave his little house—Ellie's clubhouse.

"What do I do now, Ellie?" he wondered aloud.

That night, Carl walked through the quiet house. Every single thing brought back memories of Ellie. As Carl dug his suitcase out of the closet, he found Ellie's old adventure book. Carefully, he untied the string that held it closed. He flipped through the photos of Charles Muntz and his famous blimp.

When Carl came to the page marked STUFF I'M GOING TO DO he stopped and sighed. He couldn't read any further. Ellie had never gone on her adventure. He'd promised her. He'd crossed his heart. But he'd waited too long.

Slowly, Carl closed Ellie's book. He gazed up at the mantel over the fireplace. He looked at the poster of South America, the pottery, the woven rug, the bird figurine, and the little toy blimp. But most of all, he looked at Ellie's painting of their house on the tepui.

Then he glanced at the Shady Oaks pamphlet.

As he looked up at the mantel one more time, Carl's eyes narrowed just a bit. He smiled, and then crossed his heart. He'd made a decision.

By the middle of the night, most of the block was quiet and dark. Only the Fredricksen house was bright, the lights still on. Inside, Carl worked late into the night. He had a lot to prepare.

The next morning was sunny and clear as the Shady Oaks van pulled up in front of Carl's house. Two men got out. They were nurses from the retirement home.

The nurse named George knocked on the door.

"Morning, gentlemen," Carl said, opening the door. He had a suitcase in his hand.

"Good morning, Mr. Fredricksen," George said. "You ready to go?"

"Ready as I'll ever be." Carl handed the suitcase to the other nurse, A.J. "Would you do me a favor and take this? I'll meet you at the van in just a minute. I, uh, want to say one last goodbye to the old place."

"Sure," George said, and he nodded politely. "Take all the time you need, sir."

"That's typical," A.J. muttered as Carl closed the door. He and George walked toward the van. "He's probably going to the bathroom for the eightieth time."

George eyed the lawn. It was littered with empty helium tanks. "You'd think he'd take better care of his house."

At that moment, a dark shadow fell over the van. George and A.J. looked up, and their jaws dropped. Hundreds of balloons were rising from behind the house. They shot into the air like water from a fountain. Their strings were all tied to Carl's house through the chimney. As the balloons rose, the house teetered. Then it groaned. Finally, it pulled away from its foundation and floated.

Up . . . up . . . up . . .

The floating house knocked the van, setting off the car alarm. Carl poked his head out the window and shouted triumphantly, "So long, boys!"

George and A.J. couldn't do anything but gape at what Carl had done!

The house soared over the town. People stared up, unable to believe what they were seeing. Birds flew alongside the house. Carl watched them, smiling to himself. He adjusted the compass and unfurled the sails, which were made of curtains hanging on curtain rods. They flapped and billowed in the wind.

Carl and Ellie were finally headed to South America. He kissed her photo. "We're on our way, Ellie," he said. With a happy sigh, Carl settled into his favorite chair by the fireplace.

He had just closed his eyes when he heard a knock at the door.

Carl's eyes snapped open. *A knock?*

"Huh?" He stared at the front door. For a moment, he didn't hear anything. He had finally managed to convince himself that he had imagined the knock when it sounded again.

Grumbling, Carl shuffled over to the door. He looked through the peephole. All he saw were the front porch and the clouds beyond. He threw open the door.

"Aaah!" Carl cried. Russell was clinging to the outside wall, holding on for dear life.

"Hi, Mr. Fredricksen," Russell said nervously. "It's me, Russell."

"What are you doing out here, kid?" Carl demanded.

"I found the snipe," Russell explained, "and I followed it under your porch, but this snipe had a long tail and looked more like a large mouse."

Carl rolled his eyes. *That wasn't a snipe. It was a rat! What kind of Wilderness Explorer doesn't know the difference between a rat and a nonexistent snipe?* he wondered.

"Please let me in," Russell begged.

"No!" Carl snapped. He shut the door.

Russell stared at the bright sun, the blue sky, and the white clouds drifting peacefully around him. This was the worst day ever.

After a moment, the door creaked open. "Oh, all right," Carl said reluctantly, "you can come . . ."

Russell darted inside like a bullet.

". . . in," Carl finished.

Russell panted for a moment, collecting himself. Then he looked around. "Huh. I've never been in a floating house before." It was a lot like a regular house. He walked over to the fireplace and found Ellie's drawing of the house lying on top of an open page in the atlas. "Wow, you going on a trip?" Russell asked. "'Paradise Falls: A Land Lost in Time,'" he read from the drawing. "You going to South America, Mr. Fredricksen?"

"Don't touch that!" Carl snatched the page from Russell's hand and put it in his pocket. Then he slammed the atlas shut. "You'll soil it."

"You know, most people take a plane," Russell said brightly, "but you're smart because you'll have your TV and clocks and stuff."

Russell noticed the steering rig that Carl had set up in the living room. It was made from an old-fashioned coffee grinder with a crank handle. Carl had attached it to the weather vane with ropes. "Whoa. Is this how you steer your house?" Russell asked. "Does it really work? Oh, this way makes it go right, and that way's left."

Carl stumbled through the house. The way Russell was steering was making him seasick! "Kid, would you stop with the—let go of the— knock it off!"

Carl realized that he couldn't keep Russell with him. It was too dangerous, for one thing. For another, it was too annoying.

Russell ran to the window. "Hey look, buildings!" He looked down at the office buildings and the people bustling past on the street. Everyone was busy. Nobody looked up and noticed the house flying overhead. "That building is so close, I could almost touch it."

Carl shuffled to the fireplace. Clearly, he didn't have a choice. He was going to have to pull the plug on the adventure. He'd have to land the house right where they were and send Russell home.

"I know that cloud," Russell said as he stared out the window. "It's a cumulonimbus. Did you know that a cumulonimbus is formed when warm air goes by cool air and the airs go by each other, and that's how we get lightning?"

But Carl wasn't listening. He was sawing at the balloon strings with his keys. "Stayed up all night blowing up balloons . . . for what?" he muttered. Russell was still talking. He never seemed to stop. "That's nice, kid," Carl muttered, reaching up and turning off his hearing aid.

"Mr. Fredricksen," Russell said nervously, "there's a big storm coming. It's starting to get scary." Carl was still ignoring him, so he raised his voice. "We're going to get blown to bits! We're in big trouble, Mr. Fredricksen!"

Just then, a bolt of lightning flashed outside. The light got Carl's attention. He turned his hearing aid back on. "What are you doing over there?" he demanded.

Russell pointed out the window at the dark clouds. "Look!"

Carl went to the window. "See?" Russell said. "Cumulonimbus."

Thunder rumbled outside as lightning lit up the house.

Carl gasped and ran to the steering rig. He tried to steer the house out of the dark clouds, but the storm was too strong. The wheel spun, knocking Carl backward. He fell to the floor, and Russell let out a scream.

Rain lashed the house, and thunder roared. The house shifted, and Russell went flying. He landed on his back. Plates fell from the cupboards, books spilled from the shelves. Russell jumped up and tried to hide behind an umbrella stand. His backpack slid past. "My pack!" He pounced on it.

"Gotcha!" Russell kept sliding down the hall on top of the backpack. The front door swung open. Russell was about to slide through, but the door swung shut again. Russell crashed into it.

Carl struggled to his feet as photos and pictures fell from the walls. He tried to rescue his things. He grabbed what he could and tried to secure it.

Finally, Carl collapsed into his chair, exhausted. Before he knew it, his eyes had closed.

Chapter 4

Russell poked Carl in the face. Nothing happened. He poked him again—harder. This time, Carl's eyes snapped open.

"Whew." Russell breathed a deep sigh of relief. "I thought you were dead."

Carl got up. "Huh ... wha ... what happened?"

"I steered us," Russell announced. "I did. I steered the house."

Carl felt his head. He was too groggy to understand what Russell was saying. "Steered us?"

"After you tied your stuff down, you took a nap, so I went ahead and steered us down here."

Carl went to the window and stuck his head out. For a moment, the light was too bright—he couldn't see anything. When his eyes adjusted, he realized that the house was floating over a blanket of thick fog. "Can't tell where we are," he mumbled.

Russell held up a global positioning device. "Oh, we're in South America, all right. It was a cinch with my Wilderness Explorer GPS."

Carl pulled his head back in through the window and glared at the newfangled gadget. "GP—what?"

"My dad gave it to me," Russell explained. "It shows exactly where we are on the planet." Russell made a few robot-style beeps, waving his GPS proudly. "With this baby we'll never be lost!" He threw open his hands, and the GPS sailed out the window. Russell and Carl watched as the GPS fell through the clouds.

"Oops," said Russell.

Grumbling, Carl kneeled by the fireplace to cut a few balloon strings. "We'll get you down, find a bus stop," he said. "You just tell the man you want to go back to your mother."

Russell shrugged. "Sure, but I don't think they have buses in Paradise Falls."

"There." Carl finished cutting the strings. He could feel the house begin to descend like a slow elevator. "That ought to do it. Here, I'll give you some change for bus fare."

Russell put on his backpack and the house lowered through the fog. "Nah, I'll just use my city bus pass. Whoa, that's going to be like a billion transfers to get back to my house." He and Carl headed out onto the porch. "Mr. Fredricksen, how much longer?"

"Well, we're up pretty high. Could take hours to get down." Carl caught sight of something out of the corner of his eye, but it disappeared back into the fog. "Uh . . . that thing was . . . a building or something."

Suddenly, something came up through the clouds. It was headed straight for them! "What was that, Mr. Fredricksen?" Russell exclaimed.

Carl didn't know. "We can't be close to the ground yet!"

But they were—there were rocks directly

below them. Carl gasped as the landscape came into view. It was a tepui!

Bam!

The house slammed against the rocky ground. Carl and Russell were knocked off the porch. They struggled to hold on as the house bumped and dragged across the tepui. Carl and Russell both lost their grip.

But the house kept going.

Carl chased a stray garden hose that was trailing behind the house like a tail. "Wait. Wait!" he shouted at the house. "Don't, don't. Stop!" He grabbed the hose, and it pulled him into the air. "Wait! Wait! Wait! Whoa!"

With a leap, Russell grabbed on to Carl's leg. The weight pulled the house closer to the ground.

"Russell, hang on!" Carl hollered.

"Whoa!"

The house dragged them along. They slid to the edge of the tepui and then stopped. Carl looked down. He was at the top of a steep cliff. It was thousands and thousands of feet to the bottom.

"Walk back!" Carl shouted. "Walk back!"

"Okay." Russell nodded and dug in.

"Come on, come on!"

The wind tried to carry the house over the edge. Russell pulled Carl's foot with all his strength, yanking him to safety.

Carl looked around, breathing hard. They were still surrounded by fog. All he could see was that the ground was rocky. "Where . . . where are we?"

"This doesn't look like the city or the jungle, Mr. Fredricksen," Russell said.

The wind picked up again. Russell and Carl struggled to keep hold of the house. "Don't worry, Ellie," Carl muttered. "I got it."

As the fog began to clear, Carl could see where they were. He and Russell were standing at the top of a tall, flat-topped mountain. They were surrounded by more tepuis. And across from them, less than ten miles away, was Paradise Falls.

Carl gasped in disbelief. "There it is," he

whispered. "Ellie, it's so beautiful." He pulled out Ellie's old drawing—the one with the house sitting beside the waterfall. "We made it. We made it!" Carl whooped. "Russell! We could float right over there. Climb up. Climb up!"

"You mean *assist* you?" Russell asked hopefully.

"Yeah, yeah. Whatever."

"Okay. I'll climb up!" Russell climbed over Carl, stepping on his arms and face to get to the house.

"Watch it," Carl growled.

"Sorry." Russell smiled apologetically. He'd been so eager to assist an elderly person that he'd forgotten he shouldn't step on Carl to do it.

"Now, when you get up there," Carl called, "go ahead and hoist me up! Got it? You on the porch yet?"

But Russell had barely climbed six inches. He slid down the hose, exhausted, and landed on Carl's head.

"Oh, great," Carl grumbled.

"Hey, if I could assist you over there, would you sign off on my badge?" Russell asked.

"What are you talking about?" Carl snapped.

"We could walk your house to the falls."

"*Walk* it?" Carl snorted. The boy was talking nonsense again.

"Yeah," Russell said. "After all, we weigh it down. We could walk it right over there. Like a parade balloon!"

Carl started to scowl, but then stopped. He looked up. A light breeze blew, and the house swayed slightly. He was still holding on to the hose. The house pulled him forward . . . toward the falls.

Walk to the falls. It was totally crazy . . . crazy enough to work.

Soon Carl and Russell were ready to go. They had made harnesses out of the garden hose, which they tied across their chests.

As they hiked, Carl tried to make Russell understand the seriousness of their situation. "Now, we're going to walk to the falls quickly and quietly, with no rap music or flashdancing," he explained. "We have three days, at best, before the helium leaks out of those balloons, and if we're not at the falls when that happens, we're not getting to the falls!"

But Russell was barely listening. There were so many new and interesting sights on the tepui, it was difficult to concentrate on Carl's words.

Carl looked over at the falls, then up at his house. "Don't you worry, Ellie," he muttered. "We'll get our house over there."

Dragging the house behind them was difficult work. But Russell didn't mind it. "This is fun already, isn't it?" he asked happily. "By the time we get there, you're gonna feel so assisted."

Suddenly, he had an idea. "Oh, Mr. Fredricksen. If we happen to get separated, use the Wilderness Explorer call: *Caw-caw! Rarr!*"

Carl winced as the call set off his hearing aid once more.

"Wait," Russell said. "Why are we going to Paradise Falls again?"

"Hey, let's play a game," Carl suggested. "It's called See Who Can Be Quiet the Longest."

Russell smiled—he knew how to play this one. "Cool! My mom loves that game!"

Chapter 5

Nearby, a creature blasted across a field of grass and into the cover of a grove of trees. Three dogs chased it at top speed. The prey dodged and ran, avoiding the traps that someone had set for it. It was a large, colorful bird. It couldn't fly, but it could run fast. Feathers flew as the bird burst from a grove. It came to a stop in front of a wall of rock. The bird was trapped! The dogs closed in. . . .

But in a flash, the bird leaped over the rock and escaped!

The dogs were about to follow, but a shrill whine passed nearby. It was Carl's hearing aid. The noise hurt the dogs' sensitive ears. They ran away, whimpering in pain.

"Darn thing," Carl groused as he and Russell

walked through the jungle. Carl adjusted his hearing aid again. But now it wasn't the hearing aid that was whining. It was Russell.

"C'mon, Russell!" Carl called. "Would you hurry it up?"

"I'm tired and my knee hurts," Russell griped.

"Which knee?"

Russell ignored the question. "My elbow hurts and I have to go to the bathroom."

"I asked you about that five minutes ago!"

Russell dragged his feet. "Well, I didn't have to go then! I don't want to walk anymore." He lay facedown in the dirt.

With every step Carl took, Russell was dragged a little on the ground.

"Can we stop?" asked Russell.

Carl was getting impatient. "Russell! If you don't hurry up, the tigers will eat you."

"There's no tigers in South America." Russell rolled over onto his back and pointed to a badge with a paw print on it. "Zoology," he said, and then rolled back over onto his face.

"Oh, for the love of Pete." Carl waved at the shrubbery. "Go on into the bushes and do your business."

"Okay! Here, hold my stuff." Russell handed his backpack to Carl and hurried toward the bushes. He was carrying a small shovel and a handful of leaves. "I've always wanted to try this!"

Try this? Carl thought. *Are you telling me the boy doesn't know how to go to the bathroom?*

"Mr. Fredricksen?" Russell asked after a moment. "Am I supposed to dig the hole before or after?"

"Ugh. None of my concern!"

"Oh. It's before!" Russell called.

Carl shook his head.

Russell was just about to head back toward the house when he spotted some weird tracks in the dirt. They looked almost like bird tracks. Only they were *huge*. Russell could fit three of his own feet in one footprint. "Huh? Tracks? Snipe!"

Remembering what Carl had told him, Russell clapped three times. "Here, snipe. Come on out, snipe. Sniiiiipe!"

Suddenly, the trail disappeared.

"Huh?" Russell stopped to think for a moment. He pulled a chocolate bar out of his pocket.

Something rustled in the bushes nearby.

Russell turned to look. He caught a flash of a big orange beak out of the corner of his eye—as something took a nibble of chocolate! "Gotcha!" he cried as the creature disappeared into the shrub. "Don't be afraid, little snipe. I am a Wilderness Explorer, so I am a friend to all of nature. Want some more?" Russell held out his chocolate bar.

The bird poked its beak out of the leaves and nibbled at the chocolate.

"Hi, boy." Russell's heart fluttered. He had never been this close to a wild bird before! "Don't eat it all. Come on out." The bird poked its blue-plumed head out of the shrubbery and glanced nervously at Russell. "Come on. Don't be afraid, little snipe," Russell urged. A long leg reached out of the bushes, followed by a pink and purple wing. "Nice snipe. Good little snipe." Another leg followed the first one, and the bird stood up.

Russell's eyes bugged. The bird was enormous— more than twice his height. "Nice . . . *giant* snipe!"

Russell couldn't wait to show Mr. Fredricksen! He took the bird gently by the wing and walked to where Carl was fiddling with the garden hose. He had his back to Russell.

"I found a snipe!" Russell announced.

"Oh, did you?" Carl didn't turn around.

"Are they tall?" Russell asked, looking up at the colorful bird.

Carl decided to humor the kid. "Oh, yes, they're very tall."

"Do they have a lot of colors?"

"They do indeed."

"Do they like chocolate?"

"Oh, yes . . . chocolate?" *Wait a minute. . . .*

Carl froze. Slowly, he turned around and saw Russell—standing next to an enormous bird. Carl let out a shout. "What is that thing?"

The bird chirped at Carl as if it were saying hello.

"It's a snipe!" Russell said.

"There's no such thing as a snipe!" Carl barked.

"But you said snipes eat your azaleas!" said Russell.

Carl grabbed Russell and pulled him away from Birdzilla. The bird hissed at Carl. It grabbed Russell, holding him in its wings like a baby.

"Hey!" Carl shouted as Russell giggled. "Go on, get out of here." Carl shooed the bird. "Go on!"

The bird hissed again. Then it climbed a nearby tree. It tossed Russell into the air and caught him again.

Russell laughed. "Whoa!"

"Careful, Russell!" Carl shouted—as if Russell were in charge of the situation.

"Hey, look, Mr. Fredricksen," Russell called. "It likes me!" The bird held him upside down, and his cap fell off. "Whoa!" The bird pecked lightly at Russell's hair.

"No, stop!" Russell begged. "That tickles!"

Carl poked at the bird with his cane. "Get out of here. Go on, git!"

The bird set Russell down gently at the base of the tree. Then it hissed at Carl.

"Uh-oh!" Russell hurried to Carl's side. "No, no, no, Kevin," he told the bird, "it's okay. Mr. Fredricksen is nice!" He patted Carl on the head to demonstrate.

"Kevin?" Carl asked.

"Yeah. That's his name I just gave him."

The bird patted Carl on the head with its beak.

"Beat it! Vamoose! Scram!" Carl waved his cane at the bird, but the creature ate it. Carl watched a cane-shaped bulge slide down the bird's slim neck.

"Hey!" he griped. "That's mine."

The bird coughed up the cane. It landed at Carl's feet.

Carl let out a frustrated sigh. "Shoo, shoo!" He waved at the bird. The bird waved back. Carl couldn't believe it—the bird was mimicking him! "Get out of here," Carl said. "Go on, beat it."

But the bird didn't go anywhere.

Carl threw his hands in the air. He untied the garden hose from a nearby tree and put his harness back on.

"Can we keep him?" Russell begged. Using the bird's legs as stilts, Russell walked the creature over to Carl. "Please? I'll get the food for him, I'll walk him, I'll change his newspapers."

"No!" Carl snapped.

But Russell wouldn't give up. "'An Explorer is a friend to all, be it plants or fish or tiny mole,'" he said, reciting the Wilderness Explorers motto.

"That doesn't even rhyme," said Carl.

"Yeah, it does," Russell insisted. He pointed to the roof of Carl's house. "Hey, look—Kevin!"

Sure enough, the giant bird had hopped on top of the house.

"What? Get down! You're not allowed up there!" Carl yelled.

Kevin pecked at the balloons, then swallowed one. A giant egg shape went down the bird's slender throat. *Pop!* The shape disappeared. Kevin coughed up a deflated balloon.

"You come down here right now!" Carl insisted.

Kevin slid down the hose and hid behind Russell.

"Sheesh!" Carl grumbled. "Can you believe this, Ellie?"

Suddenly, Russell had an idea. Why was Carl the only one who could talk to Ellie? "Ellie?" Russell said to the house. "Uh, hey, Ellie, could I keep the bird? Uh-huh? Uh-huh?" He looked at Carl. "She said for you to let me."

Carl looked up at the house. "But I told him no—" Suddenly, he caught himself. "I told you no!" he scolded Russell. "N-O."

Kevin let out a harsh hiss.

Muttering to himself, Carl started walking.

Pulling the house behind him was hard work, even with Russell's help. And Russell wasn't much help at the moment. He was distracted.

"I see you back there," said Carl.

Russell was walking slowly behind Carl, dropping pieces of chocolate. Kevin was following the chocolate trail—snatching up the pieces.

Carl turned back and yelled at the bird. "Go on, get out of here. Shoo! Go annoy someone else for a while."

"Hey, are you okay over there?" asked a voice.

With a squawk, the bird dashed away.

"Uh, hello?" Carl peered into the mist. Dimly, he could make out a human-shaped figure. It was standing above them, on a rock. "Oh, hello, sir. Thank goodness. It's nice to know someone else is up here."

"I can smell you," said the figure.

Carl stopped in his tracks. *That was a peculiar thing to say.* "What? You can smell us?"

"I can smell you."

Carl took another step toward the figure. Just then, the fog lifted, and he saw that it wasn't a person he had been talking to.

Russell giggled. "You were talking to a rock!"

It was true—Carl had mistaken a rock formation for the profile of a person.

Russell pointed at another distinctive-looking rock. "Hey. That one looks like a turtle!"

Carl frowned. Russell was right.

"Look at that one! That one looks like a dog!" Russell said.

Just then, the rock moved.

"It *is* a dog!" Russell shrieked.

It was, in fact, a rather sweet and goofy-looking golden retriever. And he was wearing a very high-tech collar.

"Uh, we're not allowed to have dogs in my apartment," Russell said a little tentatively.

The dog put his head under Russell's hand, so Russell gave him a little pat. Then he patted the dog again. The dog wagged his tail.

"Hey, I like dogs!" exclaimed Russell.

"We have your dog," Carl called. He figured the dog's owner couldn't be too far behind. After all, they'd just been talking to him.

Russell continued to scratch the dog under his chin, while the dog wiggled happily.

"I wonder who he belongs to," Carl muttered.

"Sit, boy," Russell said.

The dog sat.

"Hey, look! He's trained! Shake!"

The dog held out a paw, and Russell shook it.

"Uh-huh." Russell smiled. "Speak."

"Hi there," said the dog.

Carl's jaw dropped. Russell gasped.

"Did that dog just say 'hi there'?" Carl asked.

"Oh, yes," said the dog.

Carl shrieked and jumped back, but the dog just wagged his tail enthusiastically. "My name is Dug," the dog said. "I have just met you and I love you." Dug jumped up on Carl.

"What?" Carl couldn't believe it—he hoped

that his hearing aid had gone haywire.

"My master made me this collar," Dug explained. "He is a good and smart master and he made me this collar so that I may talk—*squirrel!*"

Dug froze and focused on a nearby tree. Nothing moved. False alarm. No squirrel. "My master is good and smart," Dug repeated.

"It's not possible," Carl said.

"Oh, it is," Dug replied, "because my master is smart."

"Cool!" Russell leaned over to inspect Dug's collar. "What do these do, boy?" He pushed a few of the buttons.

"Hey," Dug said, suddenly switching to a foreign accent, "would you *acuerdo contigo*?"

What's that? Carl wondered. *Italian?*

Now Dug was talking like a robot. "I use that collar to—" Russell pressed a button and Dug switched to another language. "—*watashi wa hanashimasu* to talk with—" Russell punched another switch, and Dug's voice returned to normal.

"I would be happy if you stopped."

"Russell, don't touch that!" Carl snapped. "It could be radioactive."

"I am a great tracker," Dug said. "My pack sent me on a special mission all by myself. Have you seen a bird? I want to find one and I have been on the scent. I'm a great tracker, did I mention that?"

Just then, Kevin leaped from the bushes and tackled Dug. The giant bird let out a dangerous hiss.

"Hey," Dug said happily, "that is the bird! I have never seen one up close, but this is the bird." He looked at Carl. "May I take your bird back to camp as my prisoner?"

To Carl, this seemed like a silly question, since the bird appeared to be holding *Dug* prisoner. Still—if Dug took the bird, two out of Carl's three biggest problems would be solved. "Yes! Yes! Take it! And on the way, learn how to bark like a real dog."

"Oh, I can bark." Dug let out a couple of good

barks. "And here's howling." He howled.

The bird hissed at Dug.

"Can I keep him?" asked Russell.

"No," replied Carl.

Russell clasped his hands and fell to his knees, pleading.

"But it's a talking dog!" he cried.

"It's just a weird trick or something. Come on!" Carl pulled Russell away from Dug and Kevin.

The bird followed them, and Dug followed the bird.

"Please be my prisoner. Oh, please be my prisoner," Dug said to Kevin.

Carl rolled his eyes. *What's going to follow us next?* he wondered. *A dancing hippopotamus?*

Chapter 6

A bulldog sniffed greedily at the ground, following the bird's tracks. The tracks stopped suddenly, and the dog sniffed madly. "Oh, here it is," he said after a moment. "I picked up the bird's scent." The dog's name was Gamma, and he wore a high-tech collar like Dug's.

Another dog—a rottweiler named Beta—sniffed nearby. "Wait a minute, what is this? Chocolate? I smell chocolate."

"I'm getting prunes . . . and denture cream!" Gamma narrowed his eyes. "Who are they?"

"Master will not be pleased," Beta said. "We'd better tell him someone took the bird, right, Alpha?"

Alpha sat nearby, his back to the others.

Carl Fredricksen has always wanted
to go on a big adventure.

Carl's neighborhood has been torn down
to make room for tall buildings.

Carl dreams of going to Paradise Falls
in South America.

Russell wants to earn his Assisting
the Elderly badge by helping Carl.

Carl ties balloons to his house and flies away.

People can't believe what they're seeing!

Everything is peaceful above the clouds.

Carl hears a knock at the door! Who could that be?

Russell was on Carl's porch when the house took off!

Carl decides to land so he can send Russell home.

Russell tries to tell Carl that a storm is coming.

Carl's house flies out of control in the storm.

Carl and Russell arrive in South America.

Carl and Russell pull the house toward Paradise Falls.
Their adventures are just beginning!

He was a fierce Doberman pinscher and the lead hunting dog. "No," Alpha said. "Soon enough the bird will be ours yet again. Find the scent, my compadres, and you two shall have much rewardings from Master for the toil factor you wage."

Though Alpha's commands seethed with menace, the voice from his collar came out high and squeaky.

"Hey, Alpha," Beta said, "I think there's something wrong with your collar. You must have bumped it."

"Yeah, your voice sounds funny!" Gamma agreed. He and Beta cracked up.

Alpha silenced them with a glare. "Beta. Gamma. Mayhaps you desire to—*squirrel!*"

All three dogs turned to stare at a tree. They stood stock-still, quivering with attention. Nothing moved. False alarm.

"Mayhaps you desire to challenge the ranking that I have been assigned by my strength and cunning?" Alpha finished.

Beta looked at the ground. "No, no. But maybe Dug would. You should ask him."

Gamma snickered. "Yeah, I wonder if he's found the bird on his *very special mission.*"

"Do not mention Dug to me at this time," Alpha snapped. "His fool's errand will keep him most occupied, most occupied indeed. Hahaha! Do you not agree with that which I am saying to you now?"

"Sure," said Beta, "but the second Master finds out you sent Dug out by himself, none of us will get a treat."

"You are wise, my trusted lieutenant." Alpha nosed a button on Beta's collar. A video screen flickered to life. "This is Alpha calling Dug. Come in, Dug."

The screen showed grass and rocks moving past. The camera on Dug's collar was pointed at the ground. "Hi, Alpha," Dug said. "Your voice sounds funny."

Alpha gritted his teeth. "I know, I know,"

he growled. "Have you seen the bird?"

"Why, yes," Dug said, "the bird is my prisoner now."

Gamma snorted. "Yeah, right."

But the camera shifted slightly, and a pink wing appeared on the screen. It *was* the bird! It lowered its head and hissed at the camera.

"Impossible!" Alpha snarled. "Where are you?"

"I am here with the bird," Dug said, "and I will bring it back and then you will like me. Oh, gotta go."

A boy in uniform appeared on the screen. "Hey, Dug!" Russell said. "Who you talking to?"

The screen went blank.

"No, wait!" Alpha shouted at the blank screen. "Wait!"

"What's Dug doing?" Beta cried.

"Why is he with that small mailman?" Gamma asked. To the dogs, anyone in a uniform was a mailman.

Beta looked at Alpha. "Where are they?"

Beta's collar beeped, locating Dug.

"There he is," Alpha cried. "Come on!"

The dogs blasted into the jungle. They were back on the trail.

Carl trudged along, pulling his house. The going wasn't so bad, as long as he wasn't walking against the wind. And it wasn't half as hard as putting up with that dog's constant begging.

"Oh, please, oh, please, oh, please be my prisoner!" Dug pleaded. He had latched on to Kevin's foot and wouldn't let go. The giant bird hardly seemed to notice, though. Kevin just kept plodding along, following Russell.

"Dug, stop bothering Kevin!" Russell ordered.

"That man there says I can take the bird," Dug said, nodding at Carl, "and I love that man there like he is my master."

"I am *not* your master!" Carl snapped. *Sheesh*, he thought irritably to himself, *you would think I asked this circus act to come with me.*

Finally, Kevin seemed to notice that there was a golden retriever attached to its leg. The bird stopped and tried to shake the dog off. But Dug didn't budge, so Kevin hissed at him.

"I am warning you once again, bird!" Dug said.

Kevin pecked at Dug, and the dog scrambled to attack.

"Hey, quit it!" Russell shouted.

Dug was discovering that it wasn't easy to attack a twelve-foot-tall bird. "I am jumping on you now, bird," the dog explained. It didn't do much good.

Russell waved his arms and tried to get between the dog and the bird. The group toppled to one side, dragging Russell and causing the house to wobble and tilt.

Crash!

A window smashed against a rock.

Carl gasped, looking up at the house. Ellie's clubhouse—it was being ruined!

Dug and Kevin stopped fighting. The dog looked sheepishly at Carl. He could tell his new master was angry. Shouting was always a good clue.

Carl glared at Russell, who gave him a nervous smile. "I'm stuck with you." He turned to Dug and Kevin. "And if you two don't clear out of here by the time I count to three . . ." Carl raised his cane to show that he was serious.

But Dug didn't get the threat. All he saw were the tennis balls that were stuck to the bottom prongs of the cane. "A ball!" Dug cried, leaping and bounding. "Oh, boy, oh, boy! A ball!"

"Ball?" Carl stared at his cane. That wasn't the reaction he'd been expecting. Still, it gave him an idea. Carl popped one of the balls off the end of his cane and waved it in front of Dug. "You want it, boy?"

"Yes, I do." Dug danced impatiently. "I do ever so want the ball!"

"Go get it!" Carl heaved the ball as hard as he could. It sailed down a ravine . . . and Dug streaked after it. "Oh, boy, oh, boy!" Dug gushed. "I will get it and then bring it back!"

"Quick, Russell," Carl urged, "give me some chocolate."

Russell hesitated. He was saving that chocolate for Kevin. "Why?"

"Just give it to me!" Carl snapped.

Russell pulled the chocolate bar from his pocket and handed Carl a piece.

Carl waved the chocolate. "Bird," he called. "Bird!"

Kevin looked over. Carl tossed the chocolate, and the bird chased after it.

"Come on, Russell!" Carl shouted. He hurried away as fast as he could. Which wasn't really very fast. After all, he was an elderly man pulling an entire house behind him.

"Wait," Russell said, following Carl. "Wait, Mr. Fredricksen. What are we doing? Hey, uh, we're pretty far now. Kevin's going to miss me."

But Carl kept going. He climbed over a ridge.

Finally, Carl paused and looked back. "I think that did the trick," he said to himself. He sat down on a log to rest.

But when he turned around, he came face to face with the golden retriever. The dog had the slobbery tennis ball in his mouth.

Then the bird showed up.

Dug dropped the ball in Carl's lap.

Well, that didn't work, Carl thought.

Darkness fell . . . and so did rain. Sheets of rain poured from the black sky. Every now and again, lightning flickered. It lit up the house, which was tied to a rock. Beneath it, Carl sat on a rock near a small fire as Russell tried to put up a tent. Dug was still wrapped around Kevin's leg. Both animals were asleep nearby.

"Which one's the front?" Russell asked himself as he fiddled with different parts of the tent. "Is this step three, or step five?"

Carl rolled his eyes. *Some Wilderness Explorer*, he thought.

Russell tightened something. He loosened it again. "There!" Russell got tangled in the tent poles and ropes. He frowned at one of the poles.

Carl looked away while Russell struggled.

"All done," Russell announced finally. He pointed proudly toward the tent. "That's for you!"

The tent fell over.

"Aw," Russell said. "Tents are hard."

"Wait, aren't you Super Wilderness Guy?" Carl asked. "With the GPMs and the badges?"

Russell bit his lip. "Yeah, but . . . can I tell you a secret?"

"No," said Carl.

"All right, here goes." Russell took a deep breath. "I never actually built a tent before. There. I said it."

"You've been camping before, haven't you?" Carl asked.

"Oh, never outside," Russell explained.

Carl eyed Russell's sash full of badges. "Why didn't you go ask your dad how to build a tent?"

Russell shrugged. "I don't think he wants to talk about this stuff."

"Why don't you try him sometime?" Carl suggested. "Maybe he'll surprise you."

"Well, he's away a lot," Russell explained. "I don't see him much."

"He's got to be home sometime."

"Well, I called, but Phyllis told me I bug him too much." Russell looked at the ground.

"Phyllis?" Carl repeated. "You call your own mother by her first name?"

"Phyllis isn't my mom," said Russell.

Carl looked away, finally understanding. Russell's parents must be divorced. "Oh," Carl said gently.

They both stared into the fire for a moment. Each was thinking his own thoughts.

"But he promised he'd come to my Explorer ceremony to pin on my Assisting the Elderly badge," Russell said at last. "So he can show me about tents then, right?"

Carl looked at Russell. The kid seemed hopeful, but also sad. Suddenly, Carl felt bad that he hadn't been nicer to Russell. The poor kid tried so hard. He had a sash full of badges, but he had never even been camping.

Carl thought about the pin that Ellie had given him. It was made out of a grape-soda bottle cap, but it meant the world to him. She'd given it to him because they were in an adventurers' club. But they'd never even had an adventure.

We're not so different, I guess, Carl thought, watching Russell.

The empty place on Russell's sash caught Carl's eye. Assisting the Elderly. *Has anyone ever worked so hard to get a stupid badge?* Carl wondered. He doubted it.

"Hey, uh, why don't you get some sleep?" Carl said gently. "Don't want to wake up the wild kingdom over there." He nodded at Dug and Kevin.

"Mr. Fredricksen, Dug says he wants to take Kevin prisoner," Russell said. "We have to protect him!" With a yawn, Russell lay down on the log next to Carl. "Can Kevin go with us?"

Carl sighed. "All right. He can come."

"Promise you won't leave him?" Russell asked.

"Yeah."

"Cross your heart?" Russell asked.

For a moment, Carl didn't answer. He'd only ever crossed his heart for Ellie. "Cross my heart," he said at last.

Carl glanced up at the house. The rain had stopped. The clouds had blown through, revealing a bright moon. The house was lit by its glow.

Carl looked around the camp—from Russell to Dug to the crazy-colored bird—and shook his head. At that moment, Paradise Falls seemed farther away than ever.

"What have I got myself into, Ellie?" Carl muttered.

Chapter 7

A croaking frog woke Carl the next morning. He sat up and yawned. "Morning, sweetheart," he said, staring up at the house. The balloons were starting to look a little limp. "We better get moving." Carl looked around the camp.

"Huh. Bird's gone," he said to himself. "Maybe Russell won't notice." He raised his voice. "All right, everybody up!"

Russell sat up. "Where's Kevin?" He jumped to his feet. "He's wandered off! Kevin! Dug, find Kevin!"

Dug sniffed frantically. "Find the bird. Find the bird. Point!" Dug pointed to the left.

Russell looked to the right. "Oh, look! There he is!"

Kevin was on top of the house. The bird let out a squawk.

Kevin stacked a banana on top of a large pile of food. A tomato rolled from the pile and landed at Carl's feet with a splat.

"Hey!" Carl complained. "That's my food! Get off my roof."

"Yeah!" Dug agreed. "Get off his roof!"

Kevin turned toward a large mass of rock and let out a call.

"What is it doing?" Carl asked.

Dug had spent enough time tracking the bird to know the answer. "The bird is calling to her babies," he explained.

"Her babies! Kevin's a *girl*?" Russell asked in surprise. He smiled at the thought that there were baby Kevins.

The bird called again. After a moment, Russell heard a faint peeping.

Kevin called again, and Carl tilted his head. He could hear the peeping, too.

Kevin answered the call. Then she gobbled the food and slid down the side of the roof.

"Her house is over there in those twisty rocks," Dug explained as Kevin started toward the large mass of rocks. "She has been gathering food for her babies and must get back to them."

Kevin turned to Russell. She wrapped the boy in her wings.

"Wait, Kevin's just leaving?" Russell asked in dismay.

Kevin patted Carl on the head with her beak. She hissed at Dug. Then she headed off toward the rocks.

Russell turned to Carl. "But you promised to protect her. Her babies need her. We've got to make sure they're together."

Carl looked at the rocks. They were far away— and in the wrong direction. "Sorry, Russell. We've lost enough time already. She can take care of herself. And don't you want to earn your badge?"

Russell looked after Kevin, hesitating. Then he

followed Carl. The two started walking, dragging the house once again.

Russell sniffled as he trudged along. "This was her favorite chocolate," he said, chewing on a candy bar. "Because you sent her away, there's more for you."

Carl rolled his eyes. Suddenly, he heard the nearby leaves rustle.

"Kevin?" Russell asked hopefully.

But instead, three large dogs burst through the bushes. Barking furiously, they circled Dug, Russell, and Carl.

Alpha stalked toward Dug. "Where's the bird?" he snarled. "You said you had the bird."

"Oh, yes," Dug said nervously. "Oh, yes. Since I have said that, I can see how you would think that."

"Where is it?" the Doberman demanded, narrowing his yellow eyes.

Dug looked over at Carl. "Uh, tomorrow. Come back tomorrow and then I will again have the bird."

Alpha snapped at Dug. "You lost it. Why do I not have a surprised feeling?" He stalked toward Russell and Carl. "Well, at least you now have led us to the small mailman and the One Who Smells of Prunes."

Dug lowered his head, whimpering. He hadn't meant to lead Alpha to Carl and Russell!

"Master will be most pleased we have found them," Alpha snarled, "and will ask of them many questions." He looked at Carl. "Come!"

"Wait!" Carl shook his head. "We're not going with you! We're going to the falls."

Gamma and Beta growled and barked, baring their fangs.

"Get away from me!" said Carl.

But the dogs didn't listen to him. It was clear that Carl and Russell had no choice but to follow them.

Carl looked over his shoulder and sighed. The frightening dogs were leading them away from

Paradise Falls. *This is the wrong direction*, he thought with every step. *We're going backward!*

To make matters worse, the ground was getting rockier. There were fewer trees and more twisted stones. Walking was becoming harder. And they weren't allowed to rest.

Finally, they rounded a bend. A large cave yawned in front of them.

Alpha led the group up to the cave entrance. Carl and Russell peered hesitantly inside. Glowing eyes were emerging from the darkness. It took Carl a few moments to realize that it was a pack of dogs. The glowing eyes were actually the lights on their high-tech collars.

"He approaches!" Alpha barked, and the others joined in. "He approaches! He approaches!"

A tall, shadowy figure appeared. "You came here in that?" the man asked Carl slowly. "In a house? A floating house?"

The figure stepped from the shadows. It was an old man. He stared up at the house, then started to laugh. "That's the darnedest thing I've ever seen!" He turned to his dogs. "You boys are slipping. Was it with them when you found them?"

Was what with us? Carl wondered.

Beta shook his head. "No, Master."

The man took a step forward. Carl noticed that, although the man was older, he was fit and strong. There was something strangely familiar about him. The way he stood, his leather flight jacket— everything about him gave Carl the feeling that they had met before. "Well," the man said, "this is all a misunderstanding. My, uh, dogs made a mistake."

"Mistake? I'll say it's a mistake. Your dogs just came out and assaulted us!" Carl said angrily.

"Well, you'd best hurry on your way," said the man. "The sun sets quickly around here. Good journey!" He turned on his heels and walked back into the cave.

Suddenly, Carl realized how he knew him. "Wait—" he called. "Are you Charles Muntz?"

The man hesitated. "Who wants to know?"

A thrill shivered through Carl. "Jiminy Cricket! Is it really you? *The* Charles Muntz? Could you . . . would you say it for me?" he asked.

Muntz gave Carl his famous thumbs-up. "Adventure is out there," he said.

"It's really him!" Carl shouted. "Charles Muntz! I'm so sorry I got steamed at you. My name is Carl Fredricksen."

Russell piped up. "I'm Russell!"

"You've been gone so long, I'm so glad to see you alive!" Carl shook Muntz's hand. "My wife and I, we're your biggest fans. We thought you were the bee's knees!"

Muntz perked up. "Is that so? You're a man of good taste!" He looked Carl over. "You must be tired. Hungry."

Russell's eyes suddenly lit up.

"Well, come on in!" said Muntz. "I'll give you the nickel tour."

Carl and Russell followed Muntz into the cave.

It took a moment for Carl's eyes to adjust to the darkness. When they did, he saw that he was in a giant room. An airship was tied at the far end. It was the *Spirit of Adventure*! CHARLES MUNTZ—EXPEDITION 1934 was written on the side. "Go ahead and moor your airship right next to mine," Muntz said.

Carl's grin widened as a gangplank was lowered. "We're not actually going inside the *Spirit of Adventure* itself?"

"Oh," Muntz replied, "would you like to?" He started up the gangplank.

Carl and Russell raced to catch up with him.

Carl felt giddy. *Oh, Ellie!* he thought. *Look at our adventurers' club now!*

"Not you," Beta said as Dug tried to follow Carl into the blimp.

"What do we do with Dug?" Gamma asked.

"He has lost the bird," Alpha snarled. "Put him in the Cone of Shame."

Gamma and Beta fastened the Cone of Shame

around Dug's neck. It was a giant funnel that went around his head. He looked like a doggie daffodil. Humiliated, Dug skulked down the gangplank, alone. He glanced sadly over his shoulder. He sighed and mumbled through his voice box, "I do not like the Cone of Shame."

Alpha had never liked Dug, and now he sneered with satisfaction as he pulled a lever and the gangplank clanged shut.

Chapter 8

"**W**ow!" Carl said as he poked around Muntz's trophy room. It was packed with rare treasures. "Would you look at that? Ah, Ellie. I can't believe I'm actually here!"

He chuckled as Muntz led him past weapons, statues, pottery, jewelry, and other objects from around the world.

"I see you like my collection," Muntz said. "This comforts me, as the years pass. A reminder of who I am. One can lose one's way on these mountains, and over time, one can forget."

Carl was barely listening. He was too entranced with the artifacts around him. "Oh, will you look at that!" he cried. "The Giant Somalian Leopard Tortoise!"

Just then, Alpha entered the room. "Master," he said in a squeaky voice, "dinner is ready."

"Oh, dear," Muntz said. He leaned over to fix the dog's broken translator.

"Thank you, Master," Alpha said in a deep, frightening voice.

"I liked his other voice," Russell said. He cast a nervous glance at Alpha.

Muntz laughed. "Well, dinner is served!"

Muntz fed Carl and Russell hot dogs. "My Ellie would have loved all this," Carl told Muntz. "You know, it's because of you she had this dream to come down here and live by Paradise Falls."

"It's a pleasure to have guests," Muntz said. "More often I get thieves, come to steal what's rightfully mine." Muntz picked up a lantern. He held it high so that Carl could see the hundreds of drawings, photos, and feathers that lined the room. They were all his research on one creature— the Monster of Paradise Falls.

"Beautiful, isn't it?" Muntz said, gazing upon his obsession.

Carl looked at the pictures. They seemed very familiar. In fact, it looked as if Muntz had spent decades searching for . . . Kevin.

"I've spent a lifetime tracking it," Muntz went on. "Trying to smoke it out of that deathly labyrinth where it lives . . ."

"Hey," Russell said suddenly. "That looks like Kevin!"

Muntz's eyes narrowed. "Kevin?"

"My new giant bird pet," Russell explained.

"But it ran away!" Carl added quickly. "It's gone now."

Muntz gave Carl a long, hard look. Then he walked over to a table that was covered in old flight helmets. "Carl. Those people who come here, they all have a story. A 'surveyor' making a map." He knocked a helmet to the ground with his cane. "A 'botanist' cataloging plants." Another helmet tumbled to the floor. "An old man taking his house to Paradise Falls." Muntz tossed a last helmet to the ground. It rolled to a stop at Carl's feet.

Carl didn't like where this conversation was headed. He glanced out the window. Kevin was sitting on the roof of his house! The bird had followed them into the cave. "Well, it's been a wonderful evening, but we'd better get going." Carl grabbed Russell's arm and dragged him out of the room. Muntz followed, his dogs at his heels.

Just then, a wail echoed through the cave.

"Kevin?" Russell cried.

Muntz gasped and looked out the window. "It's here."

He turned toward Carl and Russell—but they had slipped out the door! "Get them!" Muntz shouted to the dogs.

Carl and Russell darted down the gangplank. The dogs bolted after them.

"Hurry!" Carl urged as he and Russell worked to untie the house.

"I am hurrying," Russell insisted.

Just then, the house came loose. They slipped on their harnesses and ran, pulling the house as fast as they could.

A moment later, the dogs poured down the gangplank.

"They're coming!" Russell cried.

"Master, over here!" Dug called out. He showed them a side cave.

Carl and Russell darted toward it, but they weren't fast enough. The dogs were closing in on them.

Kevin leaped from the roof of the house. She picked up Russell and put him on her back. Then she scooped up Carl. She took off, dragging the house.

The bird raced through the cave, dogs hot on her heels. Kevin wove around the tall rock formations. Carl clung to her neck for dear life. Above him, balloons popped as they dragged against the rough ceiling.

Carl's eyes grew wide with dismay.

A giant rock loomed in front of them. The house slammed into it, and Russell fell to the ground. He was still tied into the hose harness. He was being pulled behind Kevin, bumping over the ground.

The dogs were right behind Russell. Alpha snapped at his heels!

Carl stabbed his cane at the dog. "Get back!"

Alpha was closing in. . . .

Suddenly, there was a rumble. Then a roar . . . and in a moment, a wave of rocks swept between the dogs and Russell. The dogs had to stop short.

Russell and Carl looked back as the bird kept running.

A golden figure wearing a large funnel stood at the top of the canyon wall. It was Dug!

"Go on, Master! I will stop the dogs!" Dug slid down the wall. He leaped into a gap between two boulders and turned to face Alpha. "Stop, you dogs!" he commanded.

Alpha lunged. He threw Dug against the wall, hard. The Cone of Shame popped off. Dug was okay, but the dogs raced through the gap.

Kevin blasted forward, then turned suddenly to the right. Russell swung out . . . over the edge of a cliff. The bird jumped over tall, narrow rocks. They were shaped like five-thousand-foot-tall candles. Russell bounced between the candlelike rocks. "Help!"

"Give me your hand!" Carl commanded. He pulled Russell back onto the bird just as they dropped to a landing.

Kevin came to a sudden stop. They were at the edge of a cliff. At the bottom was a river. "Oh, no!" Russell cried. The dogs were coming behind them. They were trapped.

Overhead, the house kept moving. Carl realized it was about to drag them forward. . . .

"Hang on to Kevin!" he shouted just as the house yanked them over the edge.

The dogs leaped after them. Gamma and Beta

fell into the river, but Alpha's teeth sank into Kevin's leg. Kevin cried out, but she managed to shake Alpha off. The dog landed in the water with a splash.

Carl let out a grunt as they landed on the other side of the canyon. He could hear distant barking as the river carried the dogs downstream.

Carl struggled to his feet, breathing hard. He checked his limbs. Nothing broken. He checked his house. No serious damage. He heaved a sigh of relief. He glanced over at Russell.

The boy was rushing toward Kevin. The bird couldn't stand up. She squawked pitifully and fell to the ground. Alpha's bite had injured her leg badly.

Russell bandaged her as well as he could with his first-aid kit. The bird tried to stand up, but she couldn't.

"No, no, no, no, no!" Russell urged. "Kevin! Stay down!" He turned to Carl. "She's hurt real bad. Can't we help her get home?"

Carl peered at the falls. If he waited much longer, the balloons would deflate. Then he'd never make it. But he'd promised Ellie—even crossed his heart.

But he'd made a promise to Russell, too.

Carl glanced at the rock maze.

"All right," Carl said to Russell reluctantly. "But we've got to hurry."

Chapter 9

Muntz glared at the three wet dogs standing before him. "You lost them?" he growled. He slammed his cane against the floor.

"It was Dug," Beta said quickly.

"Yeah, he's with them," Gamma agreed. "He helped them escape!"

Muntz groaned in frustration, then stopped suddenly. "Wait. Wait a minute. Dug . . ."

Muntz flipped a switch. It was a tracking switch, and it could trace Dug's collar anywhere.

Dug didn't even notice when the tracking light on his collar lit up. He was standing on the edge of a cliff, looking out over the rocks below and sniffing.

"See anything?" asked Carl.

"No, my pack is not following us!" said Dug. "Boy, they are dumb." He scampered back to Carl and Russell and began leading the way through the twisty rocks.

Russell and Carl followed, pulling the house. Kevin was on the front porch, resting.

Russell looked up at the bird. "You okay, Kevin?" She picked at her bandage, then settled back down.

"You know what, Mr. Fredricksen?" Russell said as they walked along. "The wilderness isn't quite what I expected."

"Yeah? How so?" Carl asked.

"It's kinda . . . wild," Russell said. "I mean, it's not how they made it sound in my book."

"Get used to that, kid," Carl answered.

"My dad made it sound so easy. He's really good at camping." Russell thought for a moment. "He used to come to all my sweat lodge meetings. And afterwards we'd go get ice cream at Fenton's. I always get chocolate, and he gets butter-brickle. Then we'd sit on this one curb, right outside, and

I'll count all the blue cars and he counts all the red ones, and whoever gets the most wins. I like that curb."

Russell looked up at Carl. "That might sound boring," he said, "but I think the boring stuff is the stuff I remember the most."

Carl thought about that. It was the same way with Ellie. What he missed most was just being with her. Looking at clouds. Cleaning the house. *That's not so weird,* he thought.

The baby birds called out. Kevin looked up and returned the call.

"Look, there it is!" Russell shouted, pointing to the rocks. He tried to run, but his tether stopped him.

Carl pulled on it to get his attention. "Hold on, Russell. Stand still."

Carl unclipped the hose, first from Russell and then from himself. Then he tied the house to a tree.

Russell helped Kevin off the porch. Then Kevin squawked and darted up the hill toward her babies. Carl, Russell, and Dug ran after her.

"Kevin! You're feeling better!" exclaimed Russell.

Carl laughed. "Look at that bird go!"

"That's it!" Russell hollered. "Go, Kevin. Go find your babies!"

Kevin was just at the entrance to the maze when a spotlight fell on her. It was Muntz! He had followed them in the *Spirit of Adventure*.

"Run, Kevin!" Russell screamed. "Run!"

Kevin ran, but a huge net shot out of the blimp. It forced her to the ground.

Kevin cried out.

Russell gasped. "Oh, no!"

Carl and Russell ran toward the bird. "Russell, give me your knife!" Carl cried. Russell handed it over, and Carl sawed at the net.

"Get away from my bird!" Muntz shouted.

Carl turned and gasped. He stopped sawing the net.

Muntz's dogs were moving toward them, and

they were dragging something behind them. It was Carl's house.

Carl froze. *Ellie's clubhouse!*

Muntz threw the lantern toward the house. The lantern broke, sending flames across the ground. The flames shot up. They licked at the bottom of the house.

"No!" cried Carl.

A balloon popped. Then another. Then more. The house sank toward the flames. The flames rose toward the house. . . .

A moment later, the house was on fire!

The bird cried out.

Carl felt his heart breaking. *Ellie's clubhouse! The house they had lived in together for more than thirty years! The floor where they had danced . . .*

He couldn't watch it burn. He couldn't.

"No!" The knife fell from Carl's hand.

The dogs swarmed toward Kevin. The bird cried out, terrified. "No!" Russell screamed as the dogs dragged Kevin up the gangplank, into the blimp.

"Careful," said Muntz as he turned and followed the dogs. "We'll want her in good shape for my return."

"Let her go!" Russell ran after the blimp as it took off. But it was no use. Russell watched as the blimp soared into the sky, taking Kevin with it.

Carl ran toward his burning house. He pulled it away from the fire and beat the flames with his jacket until they disappeared. He could feel Russell and Dug looking at him.

"You gave away Kevin," Russell said accusingly. "You just gave her away."

Carl sighed. *How can I explain that I didn't "just" give her away?* he thought. *They were burning Ellie's house!* "This is none of my concern!" he snapped. "I didn't ask for any of this!"

"Master," Dug said gently. "It's all right."

"I am not your master, and if you hadn't shown up, none of this would have happened!" Carl shouted. "Bad dog! Bad dog!"

Dug slunk away with his tail between his legs.

Carl put his harness back on. "Now, whether you assist me or not," he announced to Russell, "I am going to Paradise Falls if it kills me."

He started trudging.

Russell couldn't think of anything to do but follow.

The balloons were limp. The house dragged as Carl struggled over the rocky ground. When he looked over his shoulder, he saw Russell's harness. It was empty. Russell was following, but he wasn't assisting anymore. He was staring at the ground, his blood boiling with anger.

Finally, Carl reached the spot he wanted. He let the house settle almost to the ground, the balloons barely holding it aloft. Then he walked to the edge of the tepui. The sound of the falls pounded in his ears as they poured down the steep mountainside.

Carl took out Ellie's childhood drawing. He'd

placed her house exactly where she had drawn it.

I did it, Carl thought. *Finally. This adventure nearly killed me, but I kept my vow.*

He wondered why he didn't feel happy.

Russell walked up to Carl. "Here," he said. He tossed his Wilderness Explorer sash on the ground. "I don't want this anymore."

Carl picked up Russell's sash. Then he watched as Russell walked away and sat down on a rock. Carl turned toward his house. It was barely floating now. He could step right onto the porch.

Carl went inside. The living room was a mess. Lamps had toppled, the table was broken, books were lying on the floor.

Carl began to tidy up. He picked up his chair and stood it in its proper place. He put Ellie's chair next to it.

Finally, Carl sat down. He closed his eyes.

It was quiet. The only noise was the steady roar of the falls outside. It should have been relaxing . . . only it wasn't.

Carl opened his eyes. Everything around him was the same . . . but he felt different.

Ellie's adventure book was lying at his feet. He opened it and put Ellie's drawing carefully in its place. He looked at the page for a long time. Then he flipped to the next page, and then through the pages of newspaper clippings about Muntz and the photos of South America—Ellie's dreams.

He turned the page. STUFF I'M GOING TO DO, it read.

Carl drew in a deep breath. His fingers hovered at the edge of the page, afraid to turn it. He didn't want to see the empty pages. All the adventures Ellie never had . . . all because Carl hadn't kept his promise.

But he forced himself to look.

To his surprise, the pages weren't blank. And they weren't plastered with fantastic adventures she had dreamed up, either. Instead, they were full of pictures of their life together. There was a photo of their wedding. The two of them at Yosemite

National Park. Playing at the beach. Photo after photo . . .

Carl felt his throat tighten.

The last photo was of them together. They were old. They were sitting side by side, in their chairs. They looked happy.

Ellie had written something below the photo.

Thanks for the adventure, it read. *Now go have a new one. Love, Ellie*.

Carl smiled. Ellie had seen their simple life as an adventure. She had gotten her wish after all.

He looked over at her chair, but it was empty.

Russell's sash was lying across the arm. Carl picked it up. He gently touched the empty space and crossed his heart.

Carl hurried outside. "Russell?" he called. But Russell was nowhere in sight. Carl looked up just in time to see Russell rising into the air. He was holding a large bunch of balloons and a leaf blower as a steering device.

"I'm gonna help Kevin even if you won't!"

Russell called to Carl. He zoomed away, steering awkwardly with the leaf blower.

"No!" Carl shouted. "Russell! No!" He ran back to his house and struggled to lift it. But it was no use. The house wouldn't budge. He couldn't fly after Russell. Furious, Carl tossed a chair off the porch.

The house rose. Just a little, but it rose.

That gave Carl an idea.

Chapter 10

Carl tossed everything out of the house. Chairs, tables, dressers, dishes, shoes, hats, pictures in frames. The house rose a little, then some more.

Carl shoved the refrigerator off the porch.

Whoosh! Carl let out a whoop as the house took off into the air. Below, all his and Ellie's belongings lay strewn across the ground— including the couple's favorite comfy chairs, which now sat side by side, once again, at the top of Paradise Falls.

He rushed to the steering rig. He adjusted his direction and scanned the sky.

Knock, knock!

"Russell?" Carl cried. The door swung open, but Russell wasn't there. Instead, Carl saw a big-eyed golden retriever. "Dug!"

"I was hiding under your porch because I love you," Dug explained. "Can I stay?"

"Can you stay?" Carl cried, his heart soaring. "Well, you're my dog, aren't you? And I'm your master!"

"You are my master?" Dug barked and his tail wagged crazily. He lunged forward, licking Carl's face. "Oh, boy! Oh, boy!"

"Good boy, Dug. You're a good boy, Dug." Carl laughed and patted the dog.

Now all they had to do was find Russell.

Russell was on board the *Spirit of Adventure*. Muntz's dogs were tying him to a chair. He'd tried to sneak on board using his leaf blower, but the dogs had discovered him.

"Where's your elderly friend?" Muntz demanded angrily.

Russell's face clouded. "He's not my friend

anymore." Russell turned on the leaf blower and blasted Muntz in the face.

Muntz grabbed the leaf blower and tossed it aside. "If you're here," Muntz said, "Fredricksen can't be far behind." He grabbed Russell and dragged him toward the map room.

"Let me go!" Russell shouted. "Where are you keeping Kevin?"

Beta snarled as he leaned close to Russell. "Scream all you want, small mailman."

"None of your mailman friends can hear you," Gamma added.

Muntz looked out the porthole. A house was sailing directly toward the blimp! "Alpha!" Muntz shouted. "Fredricksen's coming back. Guard that bird. If you see the old man, kill him." He flipped a switch and walked out of the room.

The floor below Russell started to lower. He was on the ramp!

Muntz headed for the cockpit and took the wheel. The house had disappeared. "Where are you, Fredricksen?" he snarled.

Muntz didn't know that the house was behind him. From his porch, Carl could see that Russell was on the ramp, tied to a chair. Carl put on Russell's sash and then noticed that Russell was starting to slide toward the edge.

Carl steered his house closer to the blimp. He hooked his cane to the garden hose and zipped over to Russell. Just as Russell was about to slide off the ramp, Carl reached out and caught the back of Russell's chair. He scooped him to safety at the edge of the ramp.

"Dug!" Carl cried. "Bring her over!"

"Mr. Fredricksen!" Russell cried. "You came back for Kevin! Let's go get her."

"I don't want your help," Carl announced. "I want you safe." He and Dug set Russell down in the living room, where he'd be safe. Then they went back for Kevin.

The whole airship was being patrolled by Muntz's dogs. Dug and Carl sneaked through an air duct until they found the bird. She was locked in a giant cage, guarded by more fierce dogs.

"What do we do now, Dug?" Carl whispered, peeping down from the air vent in the ceiling.

But Dug didn't answer. He was too busy chomping on one of the tennis balls at the end of Carl's cane.

Tennis ball . . ., Carl thought.

He lowered himself onto the top of Kevin's cage and raised a tennis ball over his head. "Who wants the ball?" he shouted.

"Me!" The dogs hopped around in excitement. "I do! I want the ball!"

"Then go get it!" Carl tossed the ball out the door.

The dogs raced after it, shouting, "I got it!"

Carl slammed the door behind them. The dogs were locked out. Then he turned to Kevin. "Let's get you out of here," he said.

Meanwhile, back at the house, Russell was still struggling with the ropes that held him to the chair. Finally, he wriggled free! Unfortunately, at that moment his chair tipped out onto the porch . . . and over the edge.

Russell screamed as he and his chair dropped from the porch. He grasped at the garden hose, which unspooled from its caddy. The chair fell away, and Russell clung to the hose.

The wind pushed the house back toward Muntz's ship.

"Does anyone know where they are?" Muntz demanded inside the cockpit. His dogs were barking and talking madly. He could hardly understand a word.

Just then, Russell slid, squeaking, across the cockpit's window, dangling by the end of the garden hose. "Whoa!"

Muntz and Alpha gaped at him. Muntz spoke into the radio. "Gray Leader," he commanded, "take down the house!"

Seconds later, an airplane zoomed from the bottom of the blimp.

"Aaaaah! Ahh!" Russell yelled as another and then another plane joined the attack.

Muntz's dogs were the pilots!

The planes fired at the house, narrowly missing Russell.

"Aaaaah!" Russell screamed.

The planes turned to make another pass at the house. Russell struggled to climb the hose.

But Russell was on his own. If he was going to get back into the house, he was going to have to do it all by himself.

"Come on, Kevin," Carl urged. He, Dug, and the bird crept through the trophy room, looking for a way out of the airship. At that moment, Muntz emerged from the shadows. He had a sword raised over his head.

Barking, Dug lunged at Muntz and bit his leg! Muntz kicked Dug out the door and slammed it shut. Dug barked at the closed door. Suddenly,

Dug heard growling. He turned slowly.

Alpha and the rest of the pack were right behind him.

"Hi," Dug said to the snarling pack.

Inside the trophy room, Muntz lifted his sword with a growl. Carl raised his cane to defend himself.

Muntz slashed at Carl, but his sword hit a pillar instead and stuck there. Carl swung his cane and missed.

Muntz pulled his sword free. He knocked Carl to the floor. "Any last words, Fredricksen? Come on, spit it out!"

That gave Carl an idea. He spat his false teeth in Muntz's face. Muntz stumbled backward, giving Carl just enough time to recover.

Carl put his teeth back in as Muntz went on the attack. "I'm taking that bird back with me alive or dead!" Muntz yelled. He swung the sword at Carl.

Just then, in the cockpit, the dogs knocked Dug against the controls. The ship tilted, and Muntz stumbled. Carl saw his chance to escape.

"Come on, Kevin!" he cried. Carl and Kevin darted out the window. They started to climb a ladder on the side of the airship. Muntz was right behind them.

Meanwhile, back in the cockpit, Alpha faced off against Dug. "I will enjoy the killing of you now, Dug," Alpha snarled.

Dug looked around, desperate. The only thing within reach was a lamp. As Alpha lunged, Dug grabbed the lampshade and thrust it over Alpha's head, knocking loose one of the knobs on his collar.

The rest of the pack stopped and stared at him. "He wears the Cone of Shame!" said one of the pack.

Horrified, Alpha realized that the lampshade looked just like the hideous funnel he had made Dug wear as punishment. "Huh? What?" he cried, his voice once again high-pitched and squeaky. "Do not just continue sitting! Attack!"

But the dogs only laughed at him.

"Sit!" Dug commanded.

Alpha sat. The other dogs were so surprised, they sat, too. They waited for Dug's next command.

Dug was delighted. For the first time, he was the leader of the pack!

But Dug's friends were still in trouble. Outside, Russell was trying to climb the hose. His hands were about to give out. "I can't do it."

"Russell!" Carl shouted.

Russell caught sight of Carl and Kevin climbing the side of the airship.

"Caw-caw, rarr! Caw-caw, rarr!" Carl called.

The Wilderness Explorer call set Russell's blood on fire! "You leave Mr. Fredricksen alone!" he shouted at Muntz. Russell wasn't about to let a fellow Explorer down! Hand over hand, he hauled himself up to the house. He ignored the planes as they dove toward him. Russell had only one goal— to save Carl and Kevin.

A plane closed in just as Russell pulled himself onto the porch.

Russell pointed down. "Hey!" he shouted. "Squirrel!"

"Squirrel!" cried the squadron leader. "Where's the squirrel?"

"Squirrel! Where's the squirrel?" shouted the other pilots. Their planes zoomed madly as they looked around, desperate to find the squirrel.

The planes slammed into each other! The dog pilots ejected and their parachutes unfurled. They dropped safely toward the ground. A dog pilot named Omega shook his head. "I hate squirrels."

On the side of the blimp, Muntz had grabbed Carl's leg. Carl kicked him off. Muntz fell partway down the ladder but managed to grab a rung at the last minute.

Finally, Carl and Kevin reached the top of the blimp. Dug joined them.

"Russell!" Carl waved his arms at the house. "Over here!"

Russell steered the house toward his friends. Carl heaved Kevin onto the porch.

"Come on, Kevin!" Carl laughed.

As the house started to rise, Carl held tight to Dug and jumped up onto the porch. They'd made it!

But then Muntz appeared. He was standing on top of the airship holding a rifle. *Boom!* One of his bullets ripped through the balloon strings, sending half of the balloons floating into the sky. The house plunged and hit the top of the airship. Carl tumbled out.

Just then, the house started to slide off the airship. It was going to fall! Carl grabbed the end of the hose, trying to stop it.

"Russell! Get out of there!" Carl yelled.

Russell, Dug, and Kevin ran out to the porch. But Muntz fired another shot, forcing them to duck back into the house.

"Leave them alone!" Carl yelled as Muntz ran toward the house.

Muntz climbed onto the porch. The house tipped forward. Carl tightened his grip. Muntz banged on the front door with his rifle. Carl knew he had to do something.

Suddenly, he had an idea!

"Russell!" he shouted. "Hang on to Kevin! Don't let go of him!"

Russell didn't understand, but he did as he was told. Both Russell and Dug held on tight to Kevin and braced themselves.

Muntz burst through the front door. He raised his rifle.

Outside, Carl pulled a chocolate bar from his pocket. "Kevin!" he cried, waving the candy. "Chocolate!"

Kevin streaked toward the chocolate. She blasted through the front window, hauling Russell and Dug with her.

Muntz scrambled after the bird. As he leaped after her, his foot got caught on a bunch of balloons and he drifted away.

Carl had done it—he'd saved his friends! But he hadn't managed to save his house. Carl watched as it disappeared into the clouds.

Ellie's clubhouse was gone forever.

"Sorry about your house, Mr. Fredricksen," Russell said sadly.

For a moment, Carl didn't speak. He wasn't nearly as upset as he'd thought he'd be. He had thought that the house, with all its reminders, was keeping Ellie near him. But now he realized something. Ellie wasn't in the house.

Ellie was in his heart.

"You know," Carl said, "it's just a house."

He turned toward Dug, Kevin, and Russell. *They're more than friends,* Carl thought.

They're family.

And speaking of family . . .

Chapter 11

"**O**w!" Carl laughed as the baby bird pecked at his head, grooming him. He was holding another little bird in his hand.

"Look at you," Russell cooed at the babies, "you're so soft."

Kevin called out. She was at the entrance to the labyrinth—her home, where she would be safe.

Carl and Russell groaned. It was time to say goodbye. They set Kevin's babies gently on the ground and watched as they streaked toward their mother.

"I wish I could keep one," Russell said sadly.

One of the babies hissed at Dug. But Dug wasn't offended. He had finally accepted that these birds simply didn't want to be his prisoners.

Kevin cuddled her babies for a moment. Then she led them into the labyrinth. She turned back and squawked.

"Bye, Kevin." Russell waved.

Then he and Carl headed back to the blimp.

"Ready?" Russell asked as he sat at the controls.

"Ready!" Carl grinned at his copilot as they took off into the sky.

Muntz's dogs hung their heads through the open windows, enjoying the breeze. It turned out that they weren't nearly as ferocious as Muntz had wanted them to be. Now that Carl was their master, they were just regular dogs.

They were all on their way home.

"And by receiving their badges, the following Explorers will graduate to Senior Explorers," the campmaster announced. He stood at the front of the auditorium, along with the Wilderness Explorers and their fathers. "For Extreme

Mountaineering Lore. Congratulations, Jimmy." He handed the badge to Jimmy's father, who beamed proudly.

"For Assisting the Elderly . . ." The campmaster looked up to find Russell and blinked.

Russell's uniform was beat up, and his skin was tan from his time in South America. Unlike the other Wilderness Explorers at the ceremony, Russell had been on a *real* adventure.

"Russell, is your dad here for you?" the campmaster asked.

Russell peered out into the audience, where someone was making his way forward.

"Excuse me. Old man coming through." Carl climbed onto the stage. "I'm here for him," he told the campmaster.

The campmaster handed Carl the badge. "Congratulations, Russell," he said. He moved on to the other Explorers.

Carl leaned down to pin something to Russell's sash. "Russell, for assisting the elderly, and for performing above and beyond the call of duty, I would like to award you the highest honor I can bestow: the Ellie Badge."

Russell looked down. Carl had given him Ellie's grape-soda pin. "Wow."

They saluted each other. Then Russell gave Carl a hug.

"All right, I think that covers everybody. So, let's give a big Explorer Call to our brand-new Senior Wilderness Explorers!" the campmaster said.

The audience let out a wild "*Caw-caw, rarr! Caw-caw, rarr!*"

Dug and the other dogs howled in approval.

And Carl grinned, knowing that he and his friends would have many more adventures together.

Russell and Carl sat on a curb outside Fenton's. They were licking chocolate ice cream cones and watching cars go by.

"Blue one," Russell said.

Carl squinted. "Red one."

"Blue one."

"Red one."

"That's a bike," Russell protested.

"It's red, isn't it?" Carl demanded.

"Mr. Fredricksen, you're cheating."

"No, I'm not," Carl insisted. "Red one."

"That's a fire hydrant."

Carl licked his ice cream, chuckling. "Maybe I need new glasses."

Russell looked up. The blimp was parked overhead. A single blue balloon floated up and away from them. "Another blue one," he said.

Carl nodded. He wasn't about to argue. After all, it was simply a game. And it was the simple things that he and Russell liked best.